The Downstairs Bears

The Complete Stories of

The
UPSTAIRS DOWNSTAIRS BEARS

Carol Lawson

For

Will

This edition especially produced for Borders Group Inc., U.S.A. 2000
by Egmont Children's Books Limited
a division of Egmont Holding Limited
239 Kensington High Street
London W8 6SA

The Teddy Bear Hunt first published in Great Britain 2000
by Mammoth, an imprint of Egmont Children's Books Limited.
Text and illustrations copyright © Carol Lawson 2000

The Upstairs Downstairs Bears on Holiday first published in Great Britain 1997
by Heinemann Young Books and 1998 by Mammoth
an imprint of Egmont Children's Books Limited.
Text and illustrations copyright © Carol Lawson 1997

The Upstairs Downstairs Bears at Christmas first published in Great Britain 1997
by WH Books Ltd and 1998 by Mammoth
an imprint of Egmont Children's Books Limited.
Text and illustrations copyright © Carol Lawson 1997

Carol Lawson has asserted her moral rights.

The Upstairs Downstairs Bears is a registered trademark
Licensed by Gresham Licensing Limited.

ISBN 0 434 80708 7

1 3 5 7 9 10 8 6 4 2

Printed in Dubai, U.A.E.

Freddy

Henry

Alice

Henrietta

Baby Arthur

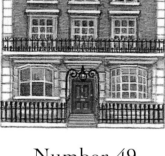

Number 49
Theodore Square

Kitty

Barker

Winston

Flora Mardle

Mrs Bumble

Polly

Nanny Maybold

The
Teddy Bear
Hunt

Today is a special day.
It is Alice and Henry's birthday.
The twins are already awake when Nanny comes in.
"Happy birthday!" says Nanny.

After breakfast, the twins open their present
from Mummy and Daddy. What a lovely surprise!

There is going to be a party but no little teddies arrive.
"Where is everybody?" says Henry.
"I don't know," says Alice.
"But look, here is a box with our names on it."

Inside the box is a roll of paper with a note attached.
It says:

Here is a puzzle,
Just for you.
To find your friends
You must solve each clue.

"It's a Teddy Bear Hunt!"
shouts Henry.

Alice unrolls the paper
and reads out
the first clue:

Thomas and Teddy
Are cosy and warm,
In a place where they know
They will come to no harm.

"They must be in bed!"
says Henry.
"Come on, let's try Mummy
and Daddy's bedroom!"

The twins run down the hallway and up the big
staircase to the landing.

They jump onto the big bed
where Thomas and Teddy are
pretending to be asleep.

"Found you!" cries Alice.

"Come on," says Henry, "let's read the next clue."
The four little bears look at the roll of paper.

Betsy and Lucy
Have come to take tea.
They are waiting politely.
Now where can they be?

"The drawing room is where the grown ups take tea,"
says Alice, and they rush back down the stairs.
Are Betsy and Lucy under the piano?
Are they behind the sofa or under a chair? No!

Henry sees the curtain twitch.
"Over here," he whispers.
Sure enough, that's where they are hiding!

Now there are six little bears
on the Teddy Bear Hunt.
"What is the next clue?" asks Betsy.

Alice unrolls the paper again
and reads out loud:

Hattie's a bear
Who likes to explore.
Look deep in the dark,
And mind how you go.

"I think I know where that is," says Henry.
"Follow me."
Down they go, through the house
until they reach a large door at the end
of a long dark passage.
"It's the cellar," whispers Teddy.

Keeping close together the friends climb carefully down into the cellar.
The steps are very steep and it's very dark.

Suddenly Lucy
squeaks.
"Aaagh!" she
cries, pointing to
a shadowy figure.
"It's a monster!"

"No, it's not," says a familiar voice. "It's me, Hattie!"
"Now we have to find Figgy," says Alice.

The seven little bears read the next clue:

Figgy's a bear
Who loves to eat.
So where do you go
When you feel like a treat?

"The kitchen of course!" they all cry.

Figgy isn't hiding. He is sitting drinking lemonade.
"We have finished the Teddy Bear Hunt,"
says Henry, "but where's the party?"

"Perhaps you should look at your last clue,"
suggests Mrs Bumble.

Henry looks at the roll of paper.

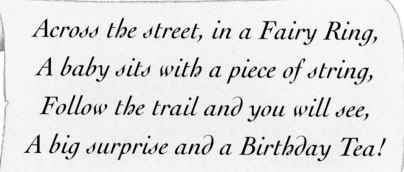

Across the street, in a Fairy Ring,
A baby sits with a piece of string,
Follow the trail and you will see,
A big surprise and a Birthday Tea!

"I know where there is a Fairy Ring," cries Alice.
"Follow me."
Mrs Bumble opens the front door and sees
all eight bears over the road and into the garden.

It doesn't take long to find Baby Arthur, asleep on a rug. Beside him is a piece of string!
"Let's see where this leads," says Figgy.

They follow the string all round the garden,
through hedges and under bushes,
past trees and flower beds, and over a little stream.

The trail ends in a sunny glade, where all the
Upstairs and Downstairs Bears are waiting.
"Surprise!" they cry.

"And there's one more surprise to come!" says Daddy.
It is Mrs Bumble, carrying an enormous birthday cake.
"Happy Birthday, Alice and Henry."

Alice and Henry blow out the candles
and make their birthday wish.
Then the eight little bears play party games
till the sky is a rosy red and it's time
for them to go home.
"That was the best party ever," says Alice.
And Henry has to agree.

The
Upstairs Downstairs Bears
on Holiday

It was seven o'clock in the morning and Henry and Alice Bosworth were already wide awake, excitedly packing their favourite toys. Today was the first day of the summer holidays and the Bosworth family were leaving 49, Theodore Square for Blossom Melbury and their house in the country.

In the nursery, Nanny Maybold was dressing Baby Arthur.

Down the passage, doing her best not to wake Mr
and Mrs Bosworth, Flora was folding dresses and shirts
in tissue paper and placing them carefully in the big
canvas trunk.

Meanwhile, in the kitchen,
Mrs Bumble was packing
a hamper of food for supper
that night and a little
something for a picnic
along the way.

Barker supervised all the travelling arrangements: Henry and Alice were going to travel with Papa and Mama and Flora and Winston in Papa's motor car. Kitty was to go by train with Polly, Nanny Maybold and Baby Arthur. The other Downstairs Bears would close up the house and follow on the next day.

As soon as breakfast was over, Winston brought the car round to the front door. Everybody climbed in and Freddy Bosworth took the wheel.

"Don't forget your hamper," said Mrs Bumble. "It's under the seat."
"And remember, twins," called Nanny Maybold, "a polite bear is a welcome bear!"

Poop! Poop! As Freddy drove slowly out of the square, a taxi cab passed him on the way to number 49.
"All aboard for Paddington station!" called the driver.

Freddy Bosworth was enjoying himself.

"Careful, Mr Frederick!" said Winston as Freddy speeded along. "We've a lot of luggage on board."

"Goodness!" shouted Henrietta, "do watch out, Freddy!"

Freddy tried to brake but the car lurched out of control and the bears found themselves rattling down a bumpy lane that ended in a shallow stream.

The engine spluttered, sighed and was silent.

"Splendid spot for a picnic, don't you think?" said Freddy, pulling off his goggles. "Help me down with the hamper, Winston old chap."

After lunch, while Freddy and Henrietta dozed in the sun, Flora and Winston took the twins down to the stream for a paddle. Flora showed them how to make paper boats and they played until it was time to set off again.

"Melbury Junction!" called out Mr Honeywig, the station master, as the London train steamed to a halt.

Kitty had already pulled down the window to look at the people waiting on the platform. "Where's Binkie?" she cried. "He promised to meet us."

"Quick, Miss Kitty, open the door," said Nanny Maybold, getting flustered. "All eyes and no action will get us nowhere."

The little group stood surrounded by luggage, and Baby Arthur began to cry, when suddenly they heard *ting-a-ling* and a small bear on a huge Penny Farthing came wobbling down the platform towards them.

"Kitty, sweetheart, it's me, Binkie! Welcome to Blossom Melbury! Oh, oh, I can't stop . . ."

Kitty watched open-mouthed as Binkie careered past them, past the ticket collector and out of the station. They heard him call faintly, "Follow me! Farmer Brewin's waiting."

It was well after six when everyone finally gathered on the lawn for a glass of Mrs Bumble's homemade lemonade.

"As a special treat we'll eat in the garden this evening," announced Henrietta.

Flora went to fetch the pie that Mrs Bumble had packed for their supper but she returned looking puzzled.

"Excuse me, Madam, but the hamper seems to be empty."

Henrietta looked accusingly at Freddy and there was a gloomy silence. Then Binkie jumped up. "Come on, Freddy," he said. "We're going fishing!"

The moon was up by the time the fishing party returned from their expedition. The bears gathered happily under the walnut tree to eat salmon and potatoes cooked on an open fire. Delicious!

"Up the wooden hill to Bedfordshire! There's another day tomorrow," said Nanny Maybold.

"It's not fair," complained Alice. "Why do we have to go to bed when everyone else is having fun?"

"Let's see what they're doing," said Henry. The two little bears crept out of bed and clambered up onto the window seat.

"Look at Binkie," said Henry, pointing to a shadowy figure in the rhododendrons. "Whatever is he doing?"

"He's serenading Kitty with his banjo!" squeaked Alice.

Having swept and polished and drawn the curtains at 49, Theodore Square, Mrs Bumble covered the furniture with white sheets. Barker checked that everything was in order, then they locked up the house and set off for the station and Blossom Melbury.

Farmer Brewin met them in his trap. "It's the Regatta on Melbury Lake this afternoon," he said as he took their cases. "Would you like to be my crew, Mrs Bumble?"

Mrs Bumble giggled. "Very kind, I'm sure," she said, "but my place is on the bank with Nanny Maybold and the little ones."

own by the lake everyone was waiting for the big race to begin. "Twice round Pirate Island, double back past Rocky Green and the first bear home is the winner!" shouted Parson Beaney. "Come on, Papa!" cheered the little bears.

"Come on, Binkie!" cried Kitty. "You can do it!"

"Well begun is half done!" said Nanny Maybold as the flotilla of little boats began to jostle for position.

Alice and Henry soon got bored with watching the boats so
Flora gave them some paper and pencils to keep them quiet.

When the race was over, the Blossom Melbury cup was presented to Binkie. "My hero!" sighed Kitty. Then there were more speeches.

"Come on, Alice," whispered Henry, "follow me."

"Nanny said we mustn't go near the water," said Alice.

"We won't," said Henry. "We'll just sit in Binkie's boat and play at being pirates."

The twins clambered aboard and soon, lulled by the rocking of the waves, they fell fast asleep.

Scrunch-bump went the boat against the jetty and *creak* went the rope that secured the *Pretty Kitty*. The twins awoke to find themselves stranded on a rocky shore.

"Henry!" exclaimed Alice, "we're shipwrecked."

"Don't panic," said Henry. "I can see Melbury harbour."

"But Henry, that means we're on the island - Pirate Island!"

"We're not scared, are we?" said Henry nervously.

"Of course not," said Alice hurriedly. "Let's explore."

Nanny Maybold looked around for the twins. Seeing no sign of them, and feeling slightly anxious, she ran to the jetty.

The first drops of rain were beginning to fall when she collided with Binkie.

"My boat!" he exclaimed. "It's disappeared."

"Oh my!" cried Nanny Maybold, "and so have the twins!"

By this time everyone had gathered on the jetty. "We'll take my boat and search the lake," said Freddy.

"My poor babies!" cried Henrietta. "You must go at once!"

Over on Pirate Island, the twins looked up at the dark sky and shivered in the cold gusts of wind.

"I don't want to play pirates any more," said Henry. "I want to go home."

Just then they saw Papa's boat passing the island. They waved and shouted but no one saw them.

"We'll have to send a message so that they know where we are," said Alice. "I know, I've got an idea!"

It was Binkie who saw the flash of white on the dark waves.
"Why, it's one of the twin's paper boats!" Freddy shouted as
he fished it out of the water. "And look, it's made out of a
Jolly Roger. That must be a clue to show where they are."
He thought hard for a moment, then . . ."Got it!" he cried.
"Steer a course for Pirate Island, Binkie old chum!" Swiftly
they turned and headed back towards the island.

Soon two bedraggled little teddies were being lifted into the *Saucy Susan*. All the bears on the jetty cheered when they saw that they were safe.

"Those naughty twins! They promised they wouldn't go near the water. They will be put to bed straight away when we get home," said Nanny Maybold sternly. "Once they are warm and dry and have had a hot drink, that is . . ."

The storm blew itself out overnight, and the next morning dawned bright and sunny. Farmer Brewin, however, was worried that the weather might break again so all the bears set off to help him bring in the harvest.

It was hard work gathering up the golden corn but everyone joined in while Barker kept an eye on things. At midday, Flora and Polly brought lunch and cool lemonade to the thirsty workers.

Suddenly there was a rumble. "Is that thunder?" said Farmer Brewin, peering around anxiously.

"Is that a rain cloud?" said his daughter Molly pointing at a large dark cloud that had appeared in the sky.

"It's Binkie!" shouted the twins.

"I've come to help," he cried over the noise of the steam engine. "Oh, oh, I can't stop . . ."

By dusk, the work was finished and all the corn was neatly stooked.

"Now, to thank you for your help," said Farmer Brewin, "you are all invited to come back to the barn for our Harvest Celebrations!"

It was nearly midnight and the harvest moon was shining brightly by the time the party was over.

"I wish we could stay in Blossom Melbury forever," said Alice, tugging on Flora's apron as they headed for home.

Flora smiled. "Well, I expect we will all be back next summer, and every summer after that, so it's almost like forever, isn't it?"

Freddy, carrying a sleepy Henry on his shoulders, led the tired but happy bears down the lane, while Kitty and Binkie lingered behind, savouring the scent of wild roses that wafted from the hedgerows.

The
Upstairs Downstairs Bears
at Christmas

It was still dark when the postman rang the bell of number 49 Theodore Square, home of the Bosworth family. Flora Mardle the parlour maid woke with a start. Christmas Eve! Shivering, she jumped out of bed, dressed quickly and ran down the two flights of stone stairs to collect the mail.

Polly the little kitchen maid and Winston the footman were already busy about the house.

Downstairs in the kitchen,
Mrs Bumble the cook was preparing breakfast
for the whole household.

Barker the butler took the letters from Flora and
strode down the hallway. In the breakfast room the
lamps were lit and the table laid ready for the
Upstairs Bears.

Freddy Bosworth unfolded his newspaper and sniffed
appreciatively. "Mmm, kippers!" he said, "my favourite!"
Henrietta, his wife, was making a list. "However will I get
everything done?" she said. "Will you order the tree,
Freddy? And Kitty, you can help Winston with the holly."
Kitty sighed and put that day's letter from her fiancé,
Binkie Bartholomew, into her pocket.

Upstairs in the nursery, the younger Bosworth
bears were having their breakfast. Nanny Maybold
was feeding Baby Arthur while Alice and Henry
finished their porridge.

The little bears were excited.
This morning they were going shopping with Nanny
and Flora, and there was the promise of a special treat.
"I'll expect best behaviour please," said Nanny.
"Remember, polite bears are welcome bears,
especially in shops."

When Nanny and Flora had bought all the things on
the list, Nanny said, "We have just one more shop
to visit before we go home for lunch."
"What kind of shop...?" asked Henry.
"...and what are we going to buy there?" asked Alice.
"Patience is a virtue," said Nanny Maybold. "Wait and see."
Holding tightly onto Flora, the twins followed Nanny
round a corner and found themselves in front of the
biggest shop they had ever seen!
Wide-eyed they went through the huge swing doors.

Suddenly a voice said, "This way if you please."
Alice turned to see a bear in a beautiful fairy costume.
She was beckoning them to follow her.
Nanny straightened Henry's scarf and
smoothed Alice's coat.
"Off you go," she said, "and remember,
tidy bears are welcome bears."
"Where is the fairy taking us?" whispered Henry to Alice.
"I don't know, but let's follow her and see," said Alice.

At the end of a long sparkly corridor the twins
caught sight of a large figure in a red robe.
"It's Father Christmas!" they gasped.

Alice didn't want to leave the toy department
but Nanny said they were needed at home so she had
to wave goodbye to the fairy and follow the others
out into the street.

On the way back Flora bought some hot
chestnuts and Henry and Alice skipped along
chattering and munching.

After lunch, Nanny sent the twins downstairs
to the kitchen with Flora while Baby Arthur had his
afternoon rest.
"Come in, come in, my dears," called Mrs Bumble
when she saw Alice and Henry.

She put the pudding basin on the kitchen table,
gave them a large wooden spoon and set them to work.
"You can never give a pudding too much stirring!"
said Mrs Bumble.
"And don't forget to make a wish."

The little bears were stirring and wishing
when the outside door suddenly flew open
and in came Winston with
a rush of cold air and snowflakes.

"Snow!" cried Henry and Alice,
"that's just what we were wishing for!"

Dressed in their warmest clothes,
the bears set off for the park.

The twins were having fun playing in the snow when
they heard a faint cry. Looking round they saw a
small figure waving to them from the top of the hill.
"Yoo-hoo! It's me, Binkie! I've got a brand new sledge
and I'm going to try it out on this slope!"

Freddy looked up. " Don't you think it's a bit..."
he began as the sledge zoomed down the hill.
"...steep?" finished Freddy, shaking his head as Binkie
and the sledge disappeared from view.
"Oh, oh, I can't stop!" shouted Binkie.

The twins were the first to reach the top of the ridge.
They saw the upturned sledge but there was no sign
of Binkie. "Where can he be?" said Henry.
Suddenly they heard a very strange growly sound.

"I think it's coming from that snowbear," said Henry
nervously. "Come on, let's take a look," said Alice.
At that moment the snowbear shook itself violently.
"It's Binkie!" cried the twins.
"That's enough sledging for me," he said. "Let's go home."

Down in the kitchen, Polly was struggling to make
long garlands of holly and ivy. She was very glad when
Kitty and the twins arrived back to help her.

Suddenly the doorbell rang.
Everyone came to lend a hand and the enormous tree
was carried into the sitting room.

Soon the house was decorated
with garlands and wreaths,
ribbons and bells, tinsel
and stars.
Only the tree remained bare.
"Won't it have some candles?"
asked Henry anxiously.
"Wait and see," laughed Freddy.
"That's what Nanny says," sighed Alice.
"Patience is a virtue!"

The twins were on their way to bed when they
heard the sound of music drifting up from the street.
"Now I wonder what that might be?"
said Nanny Maybold.

She took Alice and Henry
and Baby Arthur
downstairs and
opened the
front door.

There stood all the Upstairs and Downstairs Bears
singing carols at the tops of their voices.
"...And now it really is time for bed,"
said Nanny as the carol singers came to the end of their
concert and made their way next door.

Soon the little bears were fast asleep and
by midnight the lights at 49 Theodore Square
were out and all was quiet and still.

Henry and Alice woke to feel something heavy
on their beds - their Christmas stockings!

By eight o'clock the Downstairs Bears
were already busy.
Mrs Bumble was in the kitchen preparing vegetables.
Winston was polishing the silver
and Flora was shaking out the best tablecloth for the
dining room table.
Polly was sent upstairs to help Nanny.

Soon it was time for Nanny to take the twins and
Baby Arthur down to the drawing room.
"Knock on the door, Alice dear, and see if they are
ready for us," said Nanny.

As the doors swung open, the little bears
stared in wonder.
The tree, so green and bare yesterday, was now
hung with garlands and stars that sparkled in the
light of a hundred candles.
And beneath the tree there were presents
for everyone.

"A warm bear is a happy bear," beamed Nanny Maybold,
admiring her new shawl.

Freddy picked Alice up and held her high in the air.
"There is the rest of your present," he said.
"Can you reach it?"
"The Christmas Fairy!" cried Alice.
"She looks just like the fairy in the grotto!"
"Happy Christmas everyone!" said Henrietta.
"Happy Christmas," they all shouted in reply.

"Time for Christmas dinner,"
said Mrs Bumble.

When the pudding was finished and everyone
had congratulated Mrs Bumble on her cooking,
the fun really began.

In the drawing room the furniture was moved aside and
the carpet rolled back. They played Musical Bears and
Blind Bear's Buff, Pin the Tail on the Bear and Postbear's
Knock until they were all quite out of breath.

As night drew in and the lamps were lit at 49 Theodore Square, the Upstairs and Downstairs Bears sat sleepily together around the dying embers of the fire.
The little bears had long since fallen asleep on the hearth rug. Henry and Baby Arthur's dreams were full of games and sledging and snowbears.
But Alice smiled happily in her sleep and dreamed only of the beautiful Christmas Fairy, the best Christmas present of all.

The Upstairs Bears